# DAVID RAY

# Pumpkin Light

PAPERSTAR

The Putnam & Grosset Group

Printed on recycled paper

Copyright © 1993 by David Ray.
All rights reserved. This book, or parts thereof, may not be reproduced
in any form without permission in writing from the publisher.
A PaperStar Book, published in 1996 by The Putnam & Grosset Group,
200 Madison Avenue, New York, NY 10016.
PaperStar is a registered trademark of The Putnam Berkley Group, Inc.
The PaperStar logo is a trademark of The Putnam Berkley Group, Inc.
Originally published in 1993 by Philomel Books.
Published simultaneously in Canada.
Printed in the United States of America.
Library of Congress Cataloging-in-Publication Data
Ray, David, 1940–   Pumpkin light/David Ray.   p.   cm.
Summary: A young boy's fascination with pumpkins gets him into trouble
one Halloween. [1. Halloween—Fiction.  2. Jack-o-lanterns—Fiction.]
I. Title.  PZ7.R21012Pu  1993  [E]—dc20  92-25118  CIP  AC
ISBN 0-698-11397-7

3  5  7  9  10  8  6  4  2

For Robyn

Jacquie and Steve
at Hickory Ridge House

The morning Angus was born the sun rose like a shining pumpkin. And the light from that sun filled Angus with a light that stayed with him all his life. Angus lived on a small farm with his mother and father.

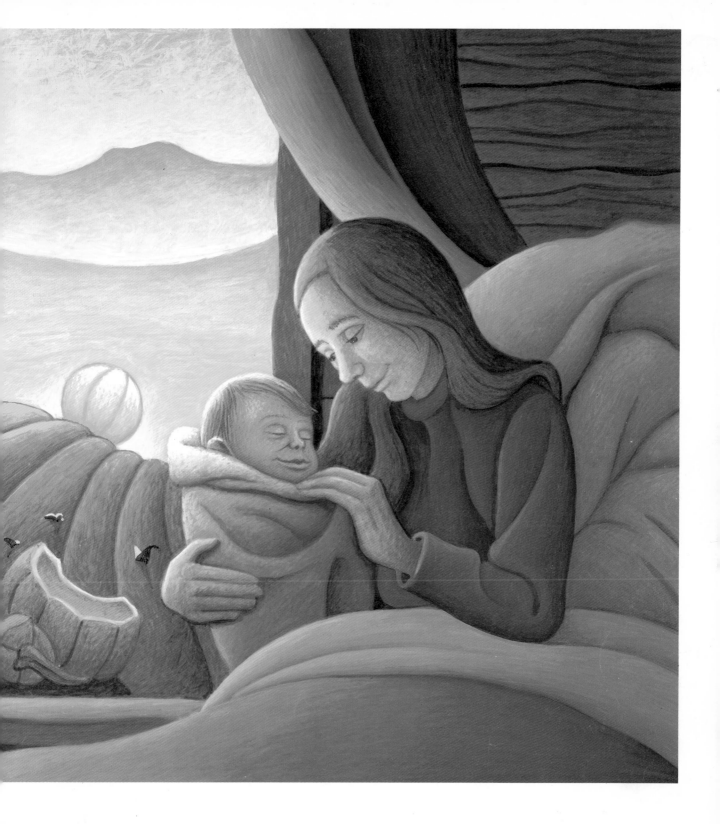

And except for his mother and father Angus loved pumpkins more than anything else. He loved pumpkins so much that he sometimes felt as if he had been hatched from a pumpkin the same as a baby chick hatches from an egg.

Every year, the day before Halloween, Angus's father went out into the field behind their barn and picked two large pumpkins. One he always carved into a jack-o'-lantern and from the other Angus's mother baked a large pumpkin pie.

Now there was one other thing Angus loved as much as his mother and father and almost as much as pumpkins and that was to draw and paint. What a wonderful time it was to sit every Halloween morning, in the warmth of the kitchen, smelling the delicious pie baking in the oven and painting pumpkin pictures in the glowing light from the great grinning jack-o'-lantern his father had carved. For Angus Halloween was a very special day.

Later in the Halloween afternoon, as October winds swirled red leaves around his feet, Angus would run the mile into town to see the general-store window. For you see, the owner of the store loved pumpkins almost as much as Angus, so on Halloween he would fill his store with jack-o'-lanterns. He put them everywhere. In the windows, on the counters, on the high and low shelves, and down on the dark shadowy floor.

Looking in from the street, Angus would see a great crowd of carved faces shining back at him. He'd stand all day and into the night in front of the window, drawing as many faces as he could before the hour came that his mother and father said he must return home.

Now, the year Angus was ten the owner of the general store carved more pumpkins than ever before, and when Angus saw them that day, he became so engrossed in his drawings that the time he was to be home was forgotten.

So the sky was dark and the moon bright when Angus gathered the finished drawings and began his long run home. The children

in the town who couldn't understand why Angus never joined them
with their trick-or-treating cried out to him as he passed by.

"Hey, pumpkin man, wadya wastin' yer time for?"

"You must be crazy."

"Look at him run. Look at him run!"

"Aw, he's just scared. We don't want him with us anyway."

Angus just ran on with his drawings under his arm. When he got home he'd hang them on his bedroom wall the way he always did, and he'd eat the warm pumpkin pie his mother would have waiting for him.

But when Angus finally did arrive home late, his mother and father were very angry.

"There will be no hanging up of drawings tonight," said his father.

"And no eating of pumpkin pie," said his mother.

"There has been just too much Halloween tonight, so it will be straight to bed for you," they both said.

Sad and hungry, Angus opened the door to his room. The walls were empty since he had already taken his old drawings down. Angus lay down on his bed and looked at the moon shining outside

his window. He began to imagine moon pumpkins floating across the sky toward the old barn loft window. He soon felt tired and fell into a deep sleep.

Though he could not have told you how it happened, he found himself high up in the barn loft. He looked out from the loft and saw his mother set a large freshly baked pie to cool on the windowsill. Seeing the pie made Angus very hungry. So he climbed down from the loft and crept up to the window and stole the pie, then ran to the cornfield and hid behind the ancient scarecrow and began to eat the pie all by himself.

"What are you doing behind my cornstalks? There was to be no pumpkin-pie-eating for you," said the angry voice of the spirit that lived in the scarecrow.

Shaking with fear, Angus turned to face the scarecrow, and the pie fell to the earth.

"I…I was hungry and didn't think Mom would mind," said Angus.

But Angus's excuse only made the spirit angrier, and he shouted at Angus. "You were told to go to bed and to eat no pie." And swinging the great scarf he wore like long arms flapping in the wind, the scarecrow turned Angus into a little dog.

"Because you now have fur the color of fallen leaves, you will be called Autumn," the scarecrow said as he made another swirl of his great scarf. "And because you stole and ate your mother's pie, every night you will climb the ladder to the barn loft and guard a magic pumpkin until a forgiving soul carves it and releases the power to change you back to a boy." The scarecrow spirit spoke in a voice as chilling as the cold which ruffled the cornstalks standing beneath him.

As Autumn ran back to the farm he tried to think of a way to get someone up to the loft to carve the magic pumpkin. But thinking is not easy when you have just been changed into a dog. So no ideas came to him.

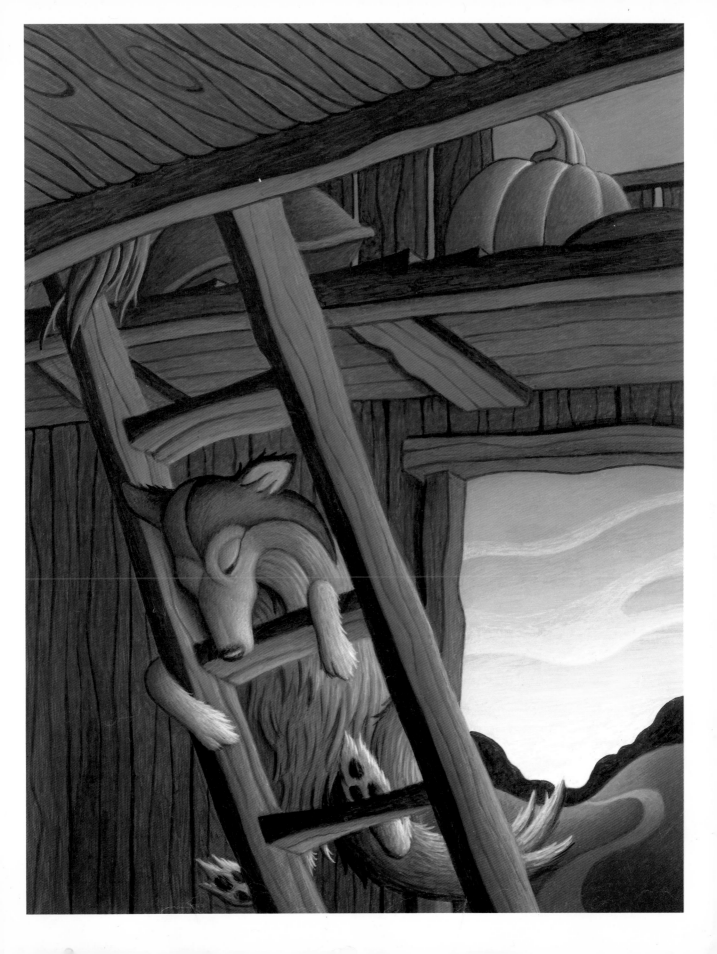

Great sadness now fell over the farm and the daily tasks were done with little joy.

"Maybe Angus just ran away," Angus's mother said in a voice full of sorrow.

"Or maybe he's been taken over the fields by an angry spirit," said his father.

"Well, at least we have *him*," the mother said, pointing to the playful little dog that had suddenly come to the farm and during the day always kept her company.

But when evening came Autumn slipped away and sadly climbed the steep ladder to the barn loft. There he lay with his head next to the magic pumpkin, guarding it through the night. Sometimes he thought he could almost hear sounds from deep within the pumpkin. As if messages from the sun and the moon somehow entered through the pumpkin's stem to rest among the silent seeds. But Angus's mother and father never came to the loft. No one did.

The long year passed slowly. Then one day, as October winds blew golden leaves around the farm, Autumn heard his mother say that even though her son was gone she would bake a pumpkin pie for Halloween. And of course she would need a pumpkin. At last an idea came to Autumn. If he could just get his mother to the barn and up to the loft she would find the magic pumpkin. Autumn began to pull at his mother's apron.

"What's wrong with you today?" cried his mother. "I have many things to do and I have no time for playing."

But Autumn kept pulling on her apron until she was out of the house and in the barnyard. Then he ran into the barn, barking louder than he ever had. His mother followed him into the barn, where it was so dark she could not see the little dog.

"Now where have you gone?" she cried.

Autumn began barking again and it seemed to come from above her. She looked up and dimly saw Autumn at the top of the loft ladder, barking wildly.

"What are you carrying on about up there? There's nothing up in that old loft."

But Autumn did not stop barking.

"All right, all right, I'll come up and take a look," she said as she began to climb the ladder. When she got to the top, the morning light lit up the corner of the loft where Autumn, smiling as much as a dog can smile, stood next to a very large pumpkin. It was one of the largest pumpkins she had ever seen.

"Now, how did this pumpkin get up here?" Of course there was no one there to answer her question except Autumn and he could not talk. So she decided to use the pumpkin for the pie she planned to bake.

She pulled at it and rolled it, and finally after a great effort she managed to get the magic pumpkin down the ladder and into the kitchen, where Autumn ran barking around the table.

"Calm down, Autumn, and let me get to work on this pie."

As she was about to cut the stem from the pumpkin, she thought of the days when her husband carved the jack-o'-lanterns for Angus.

"Well, maybe I'll just do the same."

She went to Angus's room and found one of his old drawings. She traced a jack-o'-lantern face onto the pumpkin. Then, taking a large kitchen knife, she cut into the pumpkin. When only one eye was carved, light began to shine from within. When the second eye was carved, there were streams of light. And when she carved the nose, and the smiling mouth, great shafts of light like sunbeams filled the room.

Again Autumn began to bark. But when she turned to quiet him, there, standing in the wonderful light, was her son.

The light was so bright Angus could not see. He put his hands
to his eyes and tried to rub the brightness away. Soon he could dimly
see two figures standing in the morning sunlight of his room. His

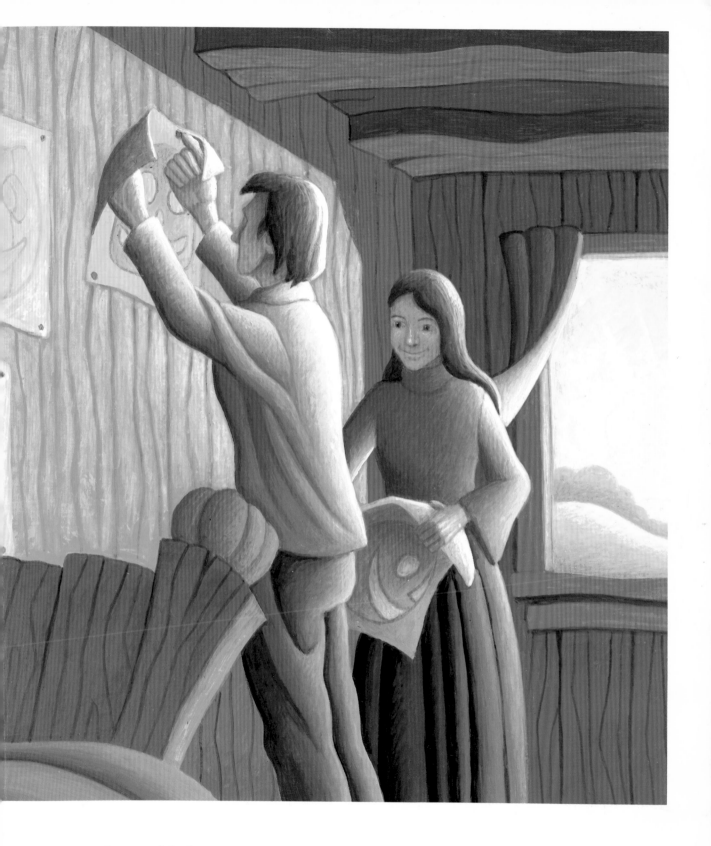

mother and father were covering the walls with his new drawings, and the delicious smell of fresh pumpkin pie came from the kitchen where they all went to eat a pumpkin pie breakfast.

The years passed by and Angus grew older, with a family of his own. And while his children sat drawing in the warmth of the kitchen, Angus painted large pumpkin paintings. Many people bought the paintings and enjoyed the warm glow they brought to their homes. Angus never stopped painting. Even when he was an old man, he worked far into the night, forgetting to do all manner of things. And when everyone in the house was asleep, he would take one last look at his favorite painting, a picture of a little dog sleeping in the glow of a pumpkin light.